W9-BRO-961

My Grandpa and the Sea

Katherine Orr

Carolrhoda Books, Inc./Minneapolis

This edition of this book is available in two bindings:
Library binding by Carolrhoda Books, Inc.
Soft cover by First Avenue Editions
241 First Avenue North
Minneapolis, MN 55401

Library of Congress Cataloging-in-Publication Data

Orr, Katherine Shelley.
   My grandpa and the sea/by Katherine Orr.
      p.   cm.
   Summary: When Grandpa, a traditional fisherman, is forced from his
livelihood because increasingly efficient technology has depleted
his island's supply of fish, he creates an ecologically sound
solution by starting a seamoss farm.
   ISBN 0-87614-409-1 (lib. bdg.)
   ISBN 0-87614-525-X (pbk.)
   [1. Fishers—Fiction. 2.Wildlife conservation—Fiction.
3. Marine ecology—Fiction. 4. Grandfathers—Fiction.] I. Title.
PZ7.0743My   1990
[E]—dc 20
                                                     89-23876
                                                        CIP
                                                        AC

Manufactured in the United States of America

        5 6 7 8 9 10 – P/JR – 01 00 99 98 97 96 95 94 93

To Chris
Carl
Kristina
and to all our friends in St. Lucia
with special thanks to Kaf

My grandpa was a fisherman on the island of St. Lucia. He had never been to school, but he was very wise. He could read the sea and sky like most of us read books. He showed me how to search the clouds for rain and taught me how sea birds can guide us to fish. But most of all, he taught me things about the heart that I will never forget.

When the weather was fine, Grandpa fished six days a week. In winter he brought home dolphin fish and kingfish that were fat and sleek, and almost as big as me. In summer he cast his nets for flying fish, which skimmed across the waves like schools of giant silver dragonflies. On Sundays, while Grammy and I were at church, Grandpa worked on his fishing boat, *Fancy Lady*.

Fancy Lady was Grandpa's pride and joy. She was carved from the trunk of a giant tree that grew high in the mountains—a real dugout canoe of the kind St. Lucian fishermen used before the days of outboard engines. Grandpa caulked her planks when they began to leak and rolled her high each day to dry, so her hull would not rot. Once each year he painted her up and down with pots of thick bright colors until she gleamed in the sun.

Grammy would scold Grandpa for not coming to church. "The wrath of God will come down upon you for not visiting His house," she would say, making her voice tremble like the preacher's at Sunday sermon.

But Grandpa would have none of it. "God is in the sea and sky, and in the fish and in ourselves. He is all about if we look and listen with our hearts. I don't need to go to a little house to meet God."

"Maybe you should come to church … just in case …," I began. But Grandpa knew what he was about.

One morning, early, he took me with him in *Fancy Lady*. We left the land behind until St. Lucia was a cutout of dark hills in a lavender world of sea and sky. Long swells lifted us gently, and the air almost held its breath. Suddenly, with a quiver of breeze, sunshine broke across the mountaintops in a river of melting gold.

"*This* is God's house," said Grandpa gently.

The following spring, Grandpa's nephew Franklin from St. Thomas came to visit us in his big, new fishing boat. He boasted about all the fish he could catch with his long lines and giant nets.

"With this boat's powerful engine and large hold filled with ice, fish can be carried for weeks without spoiling," he told Grandpa. "Times are changing, old man, and this is the way of the future. You can't compete with these new boats in that tree trunk of yours. Become my partner and we'll catch plenty. We'll grow prosperous together."

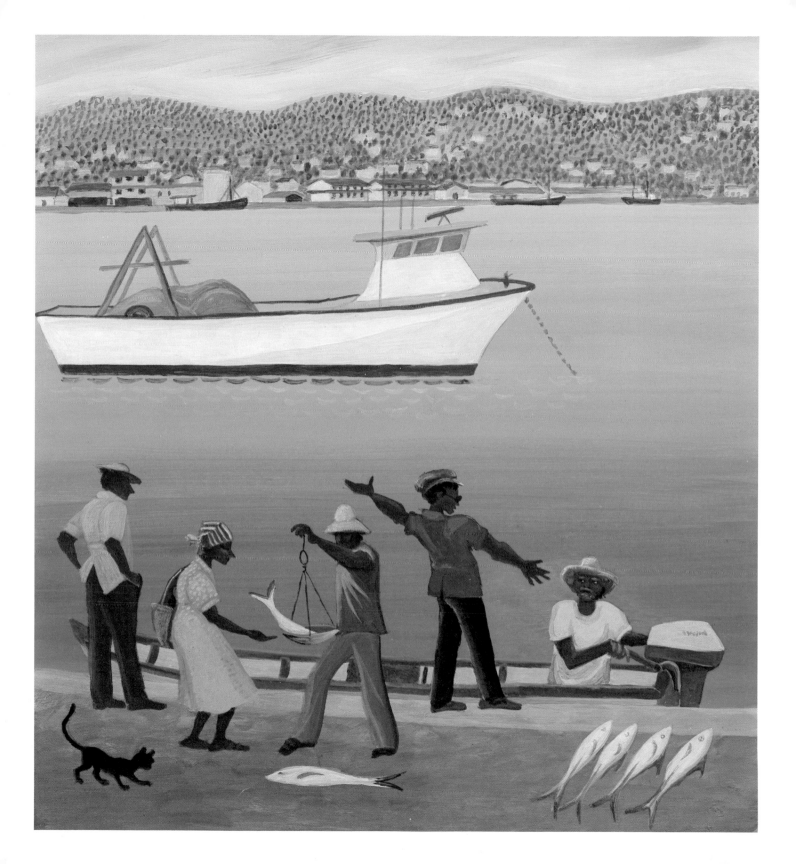

That night at supper, Grandpa chewed his food slowly and forgot to finish his fried plantains.

"Are you going to be Franklin's fishing partner?" I asked.

"Years back there were plenty of fish in the sea," Grandpa began. "Big, fancy boats like Franklin's didn't exist. But every year I see more big boats, and every year there are fewer fish left in the sea. No, I will not join Franklin. Fishermen like him are blind. They come to God's table each with a wheelbarrow instead of a plate. You cannot prosper by taking more than God can give."

"You had better clean *your* plate," scolded
Grammy as she plunked down a bowl of seamoss
pudding for dessert. Seamoss is just what it
sounds like—a mossy weed that grows in the sea.
We gathered it in slippery handfuls from among
the rocks at low tide or bought it dried at market
when we could—which wasn't often because every-
one in St. Lucia loves seamoss.

"I guess people take seamoss with a wheelbarrow
too," I told Grandpa. For even seamoss was getting
scarce.

I turned nine the year Grandpa stopped going to sea. Each year the fishing had grown worse, and that year Grandpa had not brought in enough fish to pay expenses. Grammy started a bakery. Grandpa looked for other work. He tried driving a taxi, but he said it was too hot and dusty. He tried minding the store, but he said the small space made him feel cramped.

"He's lost his heart," Grammy said. Then she sighed and boiled him up some seamoss drink. Every day she gave Grandpa seamoss drink to build up his strength because his appetite was down.

"My heart is not lost," he told me, sipping the creamy drink. "It is on the sea. There, I can feel my own place in the world within each sunset and each dawn. Here, I am stranded, like poor *Fancy Lady* when the tide is out. But surely the tide will rise and lift me again. Somewhere, Lila, there must be an answer."

He stared silently into his drink. And as I watched him, his eyes grew big and round. Suddenly he shouted, "Seamoss, Lila! Seamoss—in front of my very nose all along! The eyes are blind, but the heart sees!" He leaped up and hurried down the road, leaving his drink unfinished and me staring after him puzzling at what he meant.

Grandpa was all secrets for a week, but finally he took us to the bay where we gathered seamoss. "Look out there, Lila, and tell me what you see."

"Floating rafts?" I asked as I waded out for a closer look. They were bamboo frames with lines strung across them. Small bits of weed were tied to each line.

"If we give back something for everything we take, we will always meet with abundance," Grandpa said with shrewd, dancing eyes. "What you see, Lila, is an exchange. I'm farming seamoss."

That was the beginning. By year's end Grandpa had figured out the best spots to set out his frames. He chose places where the waves and water depth were just right, and where storms wouldn't smash his frames to bits. Grandpa determined how large to make his frames and how often to harvest the sea-moss. He trimmed off bushy fronds of moss, being careful to leave enough of a sprig to grow new fronds for the next harvest. He rinsed the cut moss in fresh water and spread it in the sun to bleach and dry. Then he packed it in bundles to sell. The new business prospered and so did Grandpa, for he was back on the sea where he belonged.

When the time came for me to go away to school, Grandpa drew me aside. "Lila," he said, "a good education will make you free to choose in life what you will. But always remember this: the head was meant to serve the heart, not the other way around."

Wherever I go in life, I shall always come home to St. Lucia. And I shall always see my grandpa, even if now he is only a memory. He will be with *Fancy Lady* in "God's house," enfolded between the sea and sky, tending his sea crops and watching the sun rise, with the waves lifting gently beneath him.

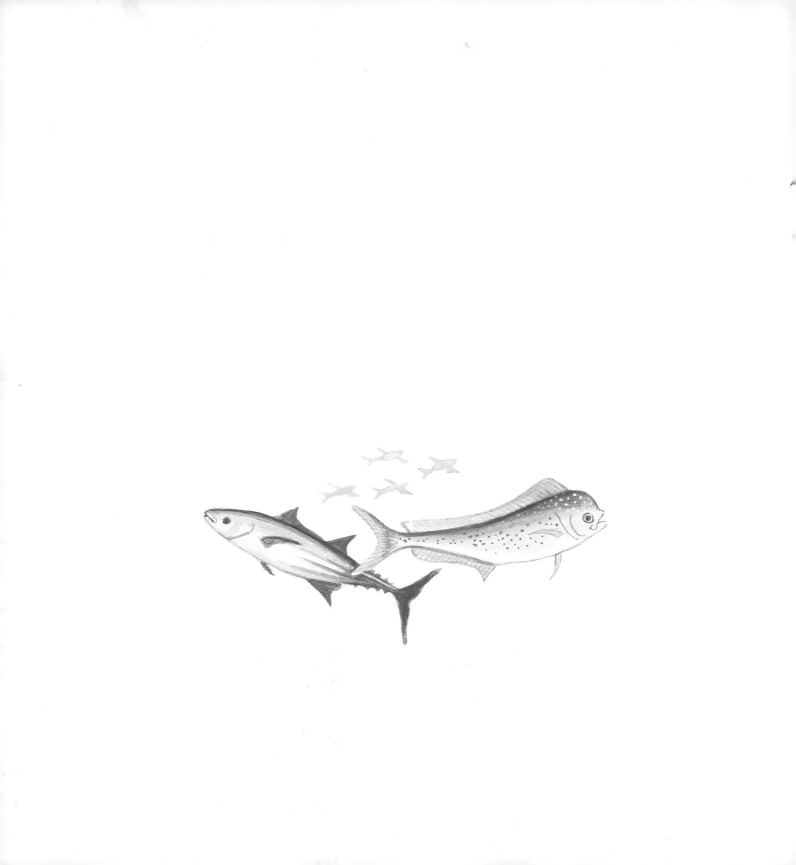